GREETINGS GAMESTERS!

Do you think Sonic is Supreme or are you a Mario Maniac? Or maybe Plumbers drive you potty, you've had it with Hedgehogs and you can't tell a Console from a sausage roll! Either way, I've got a challenge for you: My name is Zap and I've put together a Mega Collection of Game Gags and Computer Cartoons! Can *YOU* make it through all ten laughter levels? Charge up your Chuckle Circuits and find out now!

MIRTHFUL KOMBAT

Jokes with BYTE!

Written and illustrated by John Byrne

RED FOX

A Red Fox Book

Published by Random House Children's Books
20 Vauxhall Bridge Road, London SW1V 2SA

A division of Random House UK Ltd

London Melbourne Sydney Auckland
Johannesburg and agencies throughout the world

1 3 5 7 9 10 8 6 4 2

First published in Great Britain by Red Fox 1995

Phototypeset in Linotron Century Schoolbook
by Intype, London

Printed and bound in Great Britain by
Cox & Wyman Ltd, Reading, Berkshire

RANDOM HOUSE UK Limited Reg No. 954009

ISBN 0 09 941471 6

CONTENTS

LEVEL ONE

1. What's the most popular computer game in the convent?
Nuntendo.

2. Why did the dish and spoon hide their computer games?
The cat kept fiddling.

3. How did the cow feel when she scored 250,000 points?
She was over the moon.

4. What's Blue and Spiky and taken after every meal?
Tonic the Hedgehog.

5. What did Speedy Gonzales say when a bandit stole his computer games?
'Adios Amigas.'

6. What does Mario have before his alarm clock goes off?
A Nintendoze.

7. Why didn't Cinderella buy a joystick for her computer?
She's useless without Buttons.

8. 'Doctor, doctor – I keep thinking I'm a computer game.'
'Nonsense – you're just run down. Do you want me to give you some vitamins?'
'No, but I could do with new batteries.'

9. How do sharks operate computer keyboards?
They use fish fingers.

10. What do you say to Gameboys on their birthday?
'Many Zappy Returns.'

11. 'Dad really gets mad when I play computer games in bed.'
'What's so bad about that?'
'It's his flower bed.'

12. How do skunks play video games?
On their home comphewters.

13. 'Doctor, doctor, I think I'm playing too many computer games.'
'What makes you think that?'
'Well, for one thing, my nose is always running . . .'
'So what's that got to do with computer games?'
'It's running on 2 Duracell batteries.'

14. TIP FOR GAMESTERS: Take a bundle of pencils and drop them on the floor. You'll soon find yourself picking up points.

15. According to the Bible, Metheusalah lived for hundreds of years. How did he keep his gameboy working properly?
Long life batteries.

16. 'Mad hatter,' said Alice 'What's that bleeping noise coming from your teapot?'
'Haven't you ever heard of the *Nintendormouse?*'

17. 'Doctor, doctor, all these video games are tiring my eyes out.'
'Do you want them checked?'
'No, I'm quite happy for them to stay brown.'

18. 'Have you considered being a gamekeeper when you leave school?'
'Why would I want to do that?'
'Well, I'm still waiting to get back that game you borrowed six months ago.'

19. Mary had a hedgehog
Which followed her around
Till it learned to speed like Sonic
Now she's trampled to the ground.

20. 'Waiter, there's a computer game in my minestrone.'
'That's alright sir – it's Souper Mario.'

21. Did you hear about the skunk who bought an electronic table tennis game?
It went 'Ping! Pong! Ping! Pong . . .'

22. What's the highest level ghosts can reach on their computer games?
The Spirit Level.

23. Why do bottles of diluted orange score badly at computer games?
Not much concentration.

24. Who did King Arthur play computer games with?
The Bytes of the Round Table.

25. What should you wish plumbers on their birthday?
Many Tappy Returns.

26. What eats pasta, wears overalls and is always searching for Cinderella?
The Slipper Mario Brothers.

27. What did the lioness say to her cub when he beat Tarzan at Nintendo?
'I've warned you about playing with your food.'

28. Why couldn't the hedgehog concentrate on his computer game?
The other hedgehogs were needling him.

29. Did you hear about the boy who dropped his computer into quicksand?
Yes, but it didn't sink in.

30. What did one electronic game say to the other electronic game?
'How's pings with you?'

LEVEL TWO

1. What's Blue and Spiky and travels up the M1 at 200mph?
Sonic the Roadhog.

2. 'Doctor, doctor, I've swallowed some circuits from my computer.'
'I'm sorry – you've had your chips.'

3. Why should you never play games with the Pink Panther?
Because he might be a cheetah.

4. 'I'm not going back to that barber – instead of paying attention while he shaved me, he was playing a computer game.'
'What was he playing?'
'Chintendo.'

5. Why did the chicken cross the road?
To return her mains adaptor to the games shop.
Why would she want to do that?
She was a battery hen.

6. Who was playing computer games when she should have been minding her sheep?
Little Bo Beep.

7. What's the Prime Minister's favourite computer game?
Numbertendo.

8. 'How much did your new 36 bit computer game player cost?'
'A lot of money – but it's a *sixteen* bit machine . . .'
'Not since I dropped it out of the window . . .'

9. What do you do if an elephant challenges you to a game of 'Streetfighter 2'?
LOSE.

10. If you play your video games for too long, do the plumbers get tired out?
No – but they do get a little flushed.

11. Why couldn't the spinning top play with the Gameboy?
It wasn't his turn.

12. What did the button say to the computer gamer?
'Who do you think you're pushing?'

13. 'There's something wrong with my computer – all I'm getting is the same message over and over: 'WHAT'S UP DOC, WHAT'S UP DOC . . .''
'Looks like you've got bugs in your system.'

14. 'My Brother spilled superglue on his gameboy.'
'Does it still work?'
'Yes but he's stuck on level two.'

15. What's Blue and Spiky and wears a kilt?
Sonic the Hedgehaggis.

16. Knock knock
Who's there?
Amiga
Amiga Who
Am'eager to get in – hurry up and open the door.

17. Can you get a shock from computer game equipment?
Only if you look at the prices.

18. Why did the gameplayer call a plumber when his console broke down?.
Because the batteries were drained.

19. Old Mother Hubbard went to the cupboard
For a game for her four legged friend-o
But when they got there, the cupboard was bare
So the dog had to sell his Nintendo.

20. 'Waiter, there's a Sonic cartridge in my lemonade.'
'I'm sorry, sir, someone seems to have spiked your drink.'

21. What computer game do two headed monsters play?
Twintendo.

22. Why did Bugs Bunny turn up the sound on his Gameboy?
He'd lost his harephones.

23. Where do worms read about the latest computer games?
In a computer maggotzine.

24. What do goats do before buying new games for their computer?
Make sure it's compatabilly.

25. 'Doctor, doctor – my pupils play computer games all the time and the constant Beep Beep is driving me mad.'
'Come come, Headmaster, I'm sure it can't be as bad as all that. Now climb down from the staffroom roof and we'll talk about it . . .'

26. What eats pasta, wears overalls and chases big waves with a plank of wood?
The Surfer Mario Brothers.

27. Did you hear about the gamester who asked the Game Genie to make him unbeatable?
He turned into a hardboiled egg.

28. First Elephant: 'I've been looking for my Gameboy all day and I just can't find it anywhere.'
Second Elephant: 'That's because you left

it on my sofa when you came to visit yesterday.'
First Elephant: 'So why didn't you tell me where it was before?'
Second Elephant: 'I didn't think you'd want it after I sat on it . . .'

29. What's short, skinny, has a red head and likes any games which involve football?
A soccer match.

30. What computer game do spies play with?
Nintend-007.

LEVEL THREE

1. Did you hear about the gamester who lost his hand held control?
He couldn't be consoled.

2. What's Mario and Luigi's favourite party game?
Pasta Parcel.

3. What department in the computer shop do wimps head for first?
Softyware.

4. What do the Mario Brothers have for Christmas dinner?
Plumbed pudding.

5. 'Your new tennis game is really annoying me . . .'
'It's *football*, not tennis . . .'
'Well, it's making a hell of a racquet.'

6. 'When did you buy your new Simpsons game?'
'I didn't buy it – I got it for my Bartday.'

7. Who's the best games player in Gotham City?
Batteryman.

8. Why does he have to hide all his games?
Because his partner's always Robin.

9. What's sunburned, drives a jeep and travels through the jungle looking for seven foot computer consoles?
A Big Game hunter.

10. What's Blue and Spiky, blue and spiky?
Stereophonic the Hedgehog.

11. 'I like to play computer games under the blankets'
'What does your Mum say?'
'Get out of the washing machine.'

12. What's Blue and Spiky with horns and a forked tail?
Old Nick the Hedgehog.

13. What did the monster think of his new computer game?
He thought it was delicious.

14. Doctor, Doctor – my little brother's swallowed the mains adaptor for my Gameboy.'
'I'll come over straight away.'
'There's no hurry, I've got enough batteries to last till the weekend.'

15. What do hedgehogs do with ice skates and curved sticks?
Play hedgehockey.

16. What eats pasta, wears overalls and drives an ice cream van?
The Scooper Mario Brothers.

17. What computer game does Lassie play?
Rin tin tin tendo.

18. What did Mr Bean's left earphone say to Mr Bean's right earphone?
'I'm glad nothing has come between us.'

19. Little Jack Horner
Sat in the corner
Playing at 'Street Fighter Two.'
But he turned rather pale
When they threw him in jail
'Cos he'd nicked it from Little Boy Blue.

20. Why do skunks do so well at puzzle games?
Because they are fast stinkers.

21. What computer game do lifeguards play?
Swimtendo.

22. What computer game does Tom Sawyer play with?
Huckleberry Finntendo.

23. TIP FOR GAMESTERS NUMBER TWO: Get a Summer Job in a Dairy – then you'll get close to 500,000 pints.

24. What eats pasta, wears overalls and has strings coming out of its head?
The SuperMarionette Brothers.

25. 'Dad's bought me a space game as a birthday surprise.'
'How do you know it's a space game?'
'He says it's left a big space in his wallet.'

26. What's the Joker's favorite computer game?
Grintendo.

27. Why didn't the skeleton like two player computer games?
He'd no body to play with.

28. Why is Sonic a hedgehog and not a chicken?
Because otherwise, the graphics would have been fowl.

29. What's Blue and Spiky and good at fixing computer games?
Electronic the hedgehog.

30. Why did the budgie's Gameboy break down?
It was only a cheep imitation.

LEVEL FOUR

1. How do carol singers play video games?
With Comfort and Joysticks.

2. What do hedgehogs hang on the washing line?
Their Sonic-kers.

3. 'My dad fell off his ladder and landed on a pile of my computer games.'
'Was he badly hurt?'
'No – they were all software.'

4. What's Blue and Spiky and dashes through the snow?
Sonic the Sledgehog.

5. Why are weather forecasters good at computer games?
Because they've got lightning reflexes.

6. Why should you always play computer games on Feb 29th?
Because it's a bleep year.

7. What do plumbers do at the disco?
Tapdance.

8. What's round, has a hole in the middle and goes beep beep beep?
A Nintendoughnut.

9. Why do the Mario Brothers always check their drains for space aliens?
Because it's better to be sewer than sorry.

10. What did Hamlet say to the computer monitor?
TV or not TV?

11. 'Is it true that playing computer games can lead to health problems?'
'Well, Dad says he's sick of me asking him for new ones.'

12. What do you call a gorilla playing with his gameboy?
Anything you like – he's not paying attention.

13. I asked my Aunty to get me a game that involved blowing up lots of things – so she bought me two hundred balloons and a bicycle pump.

14. How do cats play computer games?
On a CD moggiedrive.

15. What's Blue and Spiky and rescues climbers stuck on mountain sides?
Sonic the Ledgehog.

16. 'The advertising for this game promises "Explosive Action" . . .'
'Well it certainly costs a bomb.'

17. Does Lassie play games on a big computer?
No – she uses a hound held console.

18. Why do Mario and Luigi play computer games?
To pasta time.

19. The Knave of Hearts thought he was smart
Till his spaceships got blown away.
Cos the Queen of Hearts had bought her own carts
And practised like mad every day.

20. What's the difference between buying cheap batteries for your computer and prunes for your dessert?
The batteries won't keep you going all night.

21. What game can you play in a very small motor car?
Minitendo.

22. Why did the Bank Manager sell his Gameboy?
He was starting to lose interest.

23. 'Teacher, teacher – tell Mark I ain't lending him my Gameboy because he ain't gonna look after it properly'
'Tsk, tsk, Paul – remember your grammar. You mean: "I'm *not going* to lend Mark my Gameboy because he *won't* look after it properly" '
'Hard luck, Mark – you ain't getting a loan of Teacher's Gameboy, neither.'

24. What eats pasta, wears overalls and is permanently bent over from carrying heavy plumbing equipment?
The Stooper Mario Brothers.

25. What game do really noisy heavy metal bands play with?
Dintendo.

26. What computer game do disc jockeys play?
Spintendo.

27. 'Batteries are so expensive, I've started to use raisins in my game instead and it works perfectly.'
'You fool – those aren't raisins. Those are electric currants.'

28. Are Polar Bears interested in computer games?
No, they leave them cold.

29. 'Can I interest you in a pocket computer?'
'No thanks – I already know how many pockets I've got.'

30. What kind of computer game do skunks play with?
A Nintend-odour.

LEVEL FIVE

1. What do you say when a big bird with a coloured beak flies off with your megadrive?
'Toucan play at that game.'

2. Have you heard about the new game called 'Escape from Prison?'
It hasn't been released yet.

3. Why does Sonic always spend New Year in Scotland?
To celebrate Hedgehogmany.

4. 'Doctor, doctor – will I be able to play computer games after I get my new glasses?'
'Of course you will.'
'Thanks very much! I could never afford a console before'.

5. 'Doctor, doctor – I keep thinking I'm a hedgehog.'
'How long has this been going on?'
'Since I stopped thinking I was a baby hedgehog.'

6. What do Vicars play on Sunday morning?
Hymntendo.

7. Why does Sonic need cheering up?
Because he's blue.

8. What computer game are toads best at?
Bleepfrog.

9. What is Mario and Luigi's favourite type of movie?
Spaghetti Westerns.

10. When do cowboys have their computer game showdowns?
At High Noontendo.

11. 'Why is your little sister sitting on the shelf between the computer game magazines?'
'Mum told her to go and join the Guides.'

12. Why did the Mummy have to take a break from his computer game?
He was getting far too wrapped up.

13. 'My new computer has a superpower memory.'
'Really? let's have a look – '
'Sorry, I forgot to bring it.'

14. 'Be careful with that computer game – someone in our local bus station got an electric shock from his console. But it was okay – he was one of the conductors.'

15. What's Blue and Spiky and very careful with money?
Economic the hedgehog.

16. What eats pasta, wears overalls and flies with the Red Arrows?
The Loop the Looper Mario Brothers.

17. 'Why aren't you playing with your new Super Realistic Football game?'
'I was, but I got sent off.'

18. Why did Mario and Luigi go to the Himalayas?
To search for the spagh – yeti.

19. Humpty Dumpty sat on the wall
Humpty Dumpty had a great fall
Where did the horses and all the king's men go?
They're all far too busy playing Nintendo.

20. What's the latest computer game craze among elephants?
Babar codes.

21. Who puts sheets over their overalls, jumps out at people and shouts 'Boo!'
The Spooker Mario Brothers.

22. What computer game do bartenders play?
Gintendo and Sonic.

23. What computer game do they play in the orchestra pit?
Violintendo.

24. What eats pasta, wears overalls and never turns up to parties?
The Pooper Mario Brothers.

25. What game do hotel managers play?
Inntendo.

26. Why shouldn't you play with your Nintendo when there are UFOs about?
You might get carried away.

27. How do wizards begin playing a computer game?
They press the on/off witch.

28. What sits on the ocean floor and plays computer games?
A Bleep sea diver.

29. What's Blue and Spiky and runs round in circles shouting 'Help Help Help'?
Panic the Hedgehog.

30. What computer game did the Octopus play with?
Nintentacleto.

LEVEL SIX

1. What's the best game to play before bedtime?
Supper Mario.

2. Why do Mario and Luigi wear their plumbers uniforms in battle?
So they can be overall winners.

3. So you've played all the Super Mario games. What do you do now?
Hope there are more in the pipeline.

4. 'Doctor, doctor – I think I'm becoming addicted to my computer game.'
'Well the first thing to do is . . .'
'Not now. Can't you see I'm about to reach level six?'

5. Who is always trying to play practical jokes on computer gamers?
Jeremy Beeple.

6. What do 30 ft gorillas use to play computer games?
Kong-soles.

7. The game shop owner suggested I look in the secondhand section . . . but I already have a second hand.

8. If dolphins are so intelligent why can't they play computer games?
They can – they just don't want to get hooked.

9. So what computer game *do* dolphins like to play?
Fintendo.

10. Why are there so many hedgehog jokes in this book?
It would be pointless without them.

11. Who plays computer games in the belfry of Notre Dame?
Quasinintendo.

12. What's hairy and hangs round game shops whenever there's a full moon?
The Softwerewolf.

13. 'I've got a new educational computer game – Mutant Ninja Killers, Part Six'
'That doesn't sound very educational to me . . .'
'Well, it's taught me a lesson about spending my money on rubbish'.

14. 'I don't know why Dad shouts so much – I've been sitting here quietly playing with my Gameboy, all afternoon . . .'
'Yes dear – but I think he'd like to use the toilet, too.'

15. What's Blue and Spiky and covered with trees, mountains and rivers?
Scenic the Hedgehog.

16. What eats pasta, wears overalls and does the backing singing for rock groups?
The Shooby dooby dooper Mario Brothers.

17. 'What did you think of that boxing game you bought?'
'I would have had more fun playing with the box.'

18. 'I see you're filing your nails again . . .'
'I have to, to be able to push the buttons on my games properly.'
'Yes – but I do wish you'd file them in someone else's cabinet.'

19. The Owl and the Pussycat went to Sea,
But the end of our story is sad
The Owl threw the pussycat over the side
'Cos her gameboy was driving him mad.

20. What kind of Christmas tree does Sonic put up?
A porcu-pine.

21. Why did Mario and Luigi go to Wales?
To fix the leeks.

22. Stan Laurel went into the computer game shop to find a new partner. Where did he look?
In the Hardyware section.

23. What did the pig say when he failed to get past level one on his computer game?
'If at first you don't succeed sty sty again.'

24. What eats pasta, wears overalls and goes round in a daze?
The Stupor Mario Brothers.

25. What's Blue and Spiky and has two horns?
Demonic the hedgehog.

26. My grandad says my computer games are too easy – he wants something he can get his teeth into.
So I brought him a glass of water.

27. How do mosquitos programme their computers?
With Insect Bytes.

28. What's Blue, Spiky and lives in Jurassic Park?
Prehistoric the Hedgehog.

29. Where do camels play computer games?
At the Nintendoasis.

30. Where is the best place in America to buy computer games?
Washington CD.

LEVEL SEVEN

1. What system does Popeye the sailor play with?
A Gamebuoy.

2. What do rubbish collectors play in their spare time?
Bintendo.

3. Did you hear about the jockey who was playing with his Gameboy while riding in the Grand National?
He was putting the cartridge before the horse.

4. How do the Addams Family play computer games?
With a skeleton keyboard.

5. What do business executives play on the 8.15 train every morning?
Commuter games.

6. What's the best game to play if you want to lose weight?
Thintendo.

7. Does Sonic have a bad temper?
No but he can be a little prickly.

8. What kind of batteries do skunks put in their computer games?
Durasmells.

9. Why do fishermen keep the sound on their computer games turned down?
They don't want to damage their herring.

10. What's the best food to eat while you're playing computer games?
Roast beep.

11. What computer game does Santa play with?
Nintendhohoho.

12. What did Julius Caesar say when he won his first computer game?
'I gamed, I scored, I conquered.'

13. What do you get if you cross an elephant with a hand held game?
Very sore wrists.

14. What computer game does Batman play with?
A ninna ninna ninna ninnentendo.

15. What computer game do you play in the nude?
Skintendo.

16. Who always beats the Lone Ranger at two player games?
Nintonto.

17. 'Some of these computer games are very difficult. I was struggling with one all last night and I finally succeeded.'
'You got to the final level?'
'No – but I managed to get the box open.'

18. What's Blue and Spiky and keeps needing to drink glasses of water?
Son-hic the hedgehog.

19. Mary, Mary quite contrary
How does your garden grow?
'It doesn't, indeed
It's covered in weeds
'cos I'm busy with Nin-ten-do!'

20. 'Doctor, doctor – I'm always pretending to be a hand held console.'
'What's your game, boy?'

21. 'What on earth are you doing?'
'I'm playing "Super Marioland" '
'But that's a ham sandwich you're holding'
'It is? Oh no – I've swallowed my gameboy.'

22. 'You wouldn't believe the price of the computer game my kid brother wants for his birthday.'

'Now, now – You should pay with a smile . . .'

'I tried to – but they insisted on money.'

23. What do you call a bad dream about computers?

A Byte mare.

24. Was Mario upset when he broke his favourite plumbing tool?
Well, it was a bit of a wrench.

25. 'I don't see how you can spend all day playing with a mindless piece of junk . . .'
'I can't help it' said the computer game. 'He's paid for me.'

26. Who do vampires play computer games with?
The kids necks door.

27. 'How much is that computer system?'
'£500 plus cartridges and tax'
'Forget the tacks – for that kind of money the cartridges should slot in by themselves.'

28. What's Red Fox's favourite computer game?
Nin-hen-do.

29. What eats pasta, wears overalls, and lives in the Swiss Alps?
The Super Mario-delayheehoo Brothers.

30. What's Mary Poppins' favourite computer game?
The Supercalifragilisticexpialidocious Mario Brothers.

LEVEL EIGHT

1. 'Doctor, doctor – I keep thinking I'm a hedgehog. Can you give me an injection?'
'I would if you'd stop rolling up into a ball . . .'

2. What's Blue, Spiky and plays guitar in U2?
Sonic the Edgehog.

3. What is the Seven Dwarfs' favourite computer system?
Nintendhihohiho.

4. And which Dwarf scores the highest?
Nintendopey.

5. What did Fingers say when the store detective found his pockets full of cartridges?
'It's a frameboy'.

6. What's Blue and Spiky and keeps stealing eggs, milk and yoghurt?
Sonic the Fridgehog.

7. What do police constables play on their day off?
Nintendelloelloello.

8. Why do hedgehogs score so highly in computer games?
They have sharp reflexes.

9. What did Mario say to his mustache?
You're starting to get up my nose.

10. What do firefighters play with when they're waiting for a call?
Flameboys.

11. What happens if you put Rice Krispies in your games instead of batteries?
The screen goes snap crackle and pop.

12. What's got fur, drinks milk and fixes leaky toilets?
The Super Meeowrio Brothers.

13. 'I've got a sore finger'
'I'm sure it's from playing too many computer games . . .'
'No – I found it outside our local butcher's.'

14. What's Blue and Spiky and picks up rubbish from the ocean floor?
Sonic the Dredgehog.

15. What computer game do acupuncturists play?
Pintendo.

16. How do budgies play computer games?
On a seedy megadrive.

17. Who wears a leather jacket, carries a whip and plays computer games in the face of danger?
Nintendiana Jones.

18. What does the Wizard of Oz use to programme his computer?
Software over the rainbow.

19. Jack and Jill went up the hill
It's really a bit of a shame
Cos Jill stuck the bucket on top of his head
And then legged it with all of his games.

20. What do undertakers play with between funerals?
A Gamebyebye.

21. Which nursery rhyme character can play computer games with all his fingers tied behind his back?
Tom Thumb.

22. Did you hear about the troop of scouts who all had gameboys?
Their motto was 'beep prepared'.

23. Why do cows play computer games?
For their own amoosement.

24. 'Did you hear about the hedgehog who wanted to go to medical school?'
'To be a doctor?'
'No – an injection'.

25. 'Mum can I put my computer game on in the car?'
'No – wear a seat belt like everyone else.'

26. 'Why are you crying, Mary?'
'My gameboy stopped working after I cleaned it with soap and water.'
'But you know water's very bad for anything electronic . . .'
'I know – but it was fine until I put it in the spin dryer.'

27. 'If you don't stop playing with that computer game I'll go crazy'.
'I think you already have – I stopped playing two hours ago.'

28. Did you hear about the computer game they made out of barbed wire?
The instructions were hard to grasp.

29. Did you hear about the milkman who sold his Gameboy?
It kept getting the butter of him.

30. Why are Barbers so good at computer games?
They know all the shortcuts.

LEVEL NINE

1. What should you give gamers on the first day of Christmas?
A Cartridge in a Pear tree.

2. What do dogs do when they need a break from playing games?
Press the paws button.

3. 'Doctor, doctor – my Uncle keeps thinking he's a plumber.'
'How is your aunt taking it?'
'She's in floods.'

4. 'Have you seen the cartoon film about the girl who kissed a Gameboy and turned it into a Handsome Prince?'
'It's called Beauty and the Beep.'

5. Where do they put people who steal computer games?
In the Son-nick.

6. What game can you play with when you're camping?
Nintento.

7. What's Blue and Spiky and pushes bunny rabbits out of their houses?
Sonic the Hutchhog.

8. Why should you never play computer games when parachuting?
You should always look before you bleep.

9. Little Boy Blue come blow your horn
There are sheep in the meadow and cows in the corn
Where was the boy who looks after the sheep?
He'd got a new Gameboy-Bleep bleep bleep bleep!

10. Why did the monster buy a bigger computer monitor?
He wanted a 36 inch scream.

11. What did the mummy monster say when baby monster spent all his pocket money on computer games?
'A ghoul and his money are soon parted.'

12. 'An elephant trampled on my computer game'
'That must be upsetting for you'
'It certainly is – I only asked him to charge the batteries.'

13. How do skunks play video games?
They connect them to their Smellyvision.

14. Knock Knock
Who's there?
Mario
Mario who?
Marry you? I wouldn't even ask you for a date.

15. How do you learn to write music for computer games?
'Nintendo-re-me . . .'

16. How do leprechauns play computer games?
On their gnome computer.

17. 'Doctor, doctor – I have this terrible urge to steal things. You've got to help me.'
'Certainly – but first, take my Gameboy out of your pocket.'

18. What computer games do giants play?
Nintendogre.

19. Twinkle twinkle little star
How I wonder what you are
It's NOT a star – I spoke too soon
It's the Gameboy that's owned by the Man in the Moon.

20. What's got wet feathers and a cartridge stuck in its beak?
A Nintenduck.

21. Monster: 'Excuse me, is the noise from my computer game annoying you?'
Passenger on Bus: 'No, not at all'
Monster: 'Right – I'd better turn it up, then.'

22. 'Doctor, doctor – my finger is sore from shooting spaceships in my computer game'
'Don't worry, I'll put on a Blastoplast'.

23. Why shouldn't you play computer games in the bath?
You might end up in hot water.

24. What's Blue and Spiky and bad for your teeth?
Sonic the Fudgehog.

25. What eats pasta, wears overalls and sits around the house all day?
The Sofa Mario Brothers.

26. What game do chiropodists play?
Nintentoe.

27. What's Blue and Spiky and used for really tough cleaning jobs?
Carbolic the Hedgehog.

28. Why did the monster smash up his Gameboy?
He'd lost his Nintemper.

29. 'Hi there – I'm a battery compartment'
'Is that a good job, then?'
'Well there are plenty of openings'

30. I went to the games shop to get a copy of 'Ninja Dragons 2' for my big brother . . . but they said they don't do swops.

LEVEL TEN

1. What system do dentists play with?
Gumboys.

2. What is the plumbers' favourite TV show?
Loo Peter.

3. What's the most popular system in Wales?
The Gameboyo.

4. What's the most popular game with whales?
The Super Mario Blubbers.

5. Why are the games in Long John Silver's shop of such bad quality?
He only sells pirate cartridges.

6. 'Bing Crosby must have asked Santa for lots of computer games'
'How do you know?'
'He's dreaming of a Byte Christmas.'

7. Which computer game builds up your muscles?
Gymtendo.

8. What did Mrs Christian Anderson buy her son for his birthday?
A Hans held game.

9. Who can't play computer games after midnight?
Nintendorella.

10. Why did Mr Bean iron his computer game?
He wanted to press the buttons.

11. What's the difference between a computer game and a slushy romance novel?
One is exciting and the other is yecch writing.

12. What's Blue, Spiky and 65 million years old?
Jurassic the Hedgehog.

13. What has horns, udders and a complete set of wrenches?
The Super Moo-rio Brothers.

14. What wears overalls, eats pasta and is always interested in someone else's business?
The Snooper Mario Brothers.

15. Which TV Channel has the most computer game reviews?
The Beepbeep C.

16. What's furry, likes honey and just made it to level 10?
Winnie the phew!

17. 'Do you like challenging computer games?'
'Yes – why do you ask?'
'Because you'll find your new one hard to play with after what the cat's done to it.'

18. What computer game do grannies play?
Nantendo.

19. Old King Cole was a clever old soul
As one fiddler said to the others
When the pipe that he'd called for was leaky
He sent for the Mario Brothers.

20. 'Doctor, doctor – my brother thinks he's a Gameboy'
'My goodness – I'd better look at him at once'
'Too late – we traded him in for a CD megadrive.'

21. 'What are you complaining for now, Mum? I locked my computer game in the toybox like you told me.'
'Yes – but you could have waited until your little brother had let go of it.'

22. What do elephants do with computer games?
Connect them to their ellyvisions.

23. Who patrols computer game shops after they've closed?
The Bytewatchman.

24. What's Blue and Spiky and plays classical music?
Philharmonic the hedgehog.

25. What game can you play if you put a toad in your mega drive?
Bleepfrog.

26. 'Since I bought my computer game I don't eat, I don't drink – I don't even sleep.'
'Why not?'
'I haven't any money left'.

27. What do computer witches have at the end of their noses?
Gameboils.

28. What did the crook say when he threw his computer console into the air?
'The game's up'.

29. What's Blue and Spiky, eats pasta, wears overalls and turns up at the end of Computer Game Joke Books?
So-long the Hedgehog and the Mari-over Brothers.

30. What has a beak, feathers and plays computer games so much, it's ended up extinct?
The Nintendodo.

Other great reads from ***Red Fox***

Giggle and groan with a Red Fox humour book!

Nutty, naughty and quite quite mad, the Red Fox humour list has a range of the silliest titles you're likely to see on a bookshelf! Check out some of our weird and wonderful books and we promise you'll have a ribticklingly good read!

MIAOW! THE CAT JOKE BOOK – Susan Abbott

Be a cool cat and paws here for the purrfect joke! Get your claws into this collection of howlers all about our furry friends that will have you feline like a grinning Cheshire Cat!

ISBN 0 09 998460 1 £1.99

THE SMELLY SOCKS JOKE BOOK – Susan Abbott

Hold your nose . . . here comes the funniest and foulest joke book you're likely to read for a while! Packed with pungent puns and reeking with revolting riddles, this one is guaranteed to leave you gasping for air!

ISBN 0 09 956270 7 £1.99

TUTANKHAMUN IS A BIT OF A MUMMY'S BOY – Michael Coleman

Have you ever dreaded taking home your school report or a letter from the Head? You're in good company! Did you know that Shakespeare was really "hopeless at English" and that Christopher Columbus had "absolutely no sense of direction"? There's fifty other previously unpublished school reports which reveal hilarious secrets about the famous which not many people know . . .

ISBN 0 09 988180 2 £2.99

THE FISH AND CHIPS JOKE BOOK – Ian Rylett

This book comes complete with a fish-and-chips scratch and sniff panel so you can sniff while you snigger at this delicious collection of piping-hot pottiness! Your tastebuds will be tickled no end with this mouth-watering concoction of tasty gags so tuck into a copy today! It's a feast of fun!

ISBN 0 09 995040 5 £2.99